A LITTLE CALM SPOT

A STORY ABOUT YOGA AND FEELING FOCUSED

Written & Illustrated
by Diane Alber

To my children, Ryan and Anna.

All inquiries about this book can be sent to the author at
info@dianealber.com
Published in the United States by Diane Alber Art LLC
For more information, or to book an event, visit our website:
www.dianealber.com
ISBN: 978-1-951287-43-6
Paperback

Printed in China

This CALM book belongs to:

_____

_____

_____

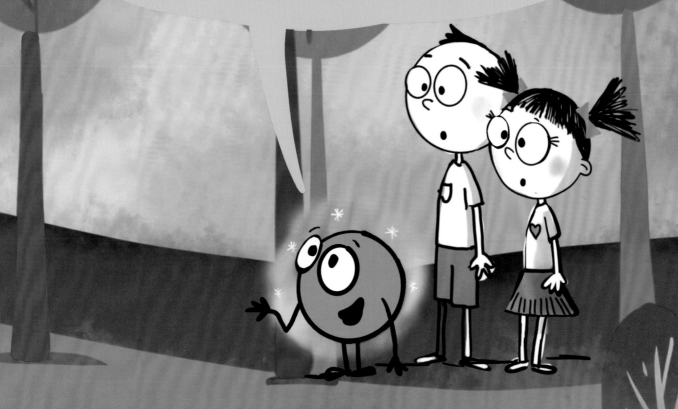

Notice how those red and gray lines are very tangled and jumpy. BIG EMOTIONS can trick your BRAIN into thinking that you don't have enough air.

You can start to BREATHE SUPER FAST, and that doesn't make you feel very good. It also makes it hard to find your PEACEFUL SPOT!

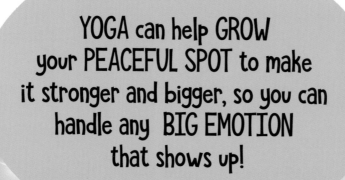

YOGA can help GROW
your PEACEFUL SPOT to make
it stronger and bigger, so you can
handle any BIG EMOTION
that shows up!

MINDSET is another part of YOGA. You can CALM your MIND by saying POSITIVE WORDS or thinking POSITIVE THOUGHTS.

Step one: BREATHE IN to smell a flower. BREATHE OUT to blow a bubble.

Step two: MOVE into a pose and continue to slowly BREATHE IN and BREATHE OUT. This is a warrior pose. It can help your back get stronger so you can stand up tall.

Step three: Think POSITIVE THOUGHTS.

I can be like a warrior and fight off any negative thoughts that enter my mind.

I can bring joy like a rainbow.

I can be wise like an owl and look
at the positive side of things!

I can be carefree like a cow.

I can stretch like a cat.

I can slow down like a snail and CALM my energy.

I can be alert like a dog!

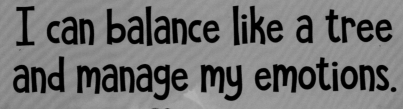

I can balance like a tree
and manage my emotions.

I can handle change
like a butterfly.

I can stand tall and confident like a mountain!

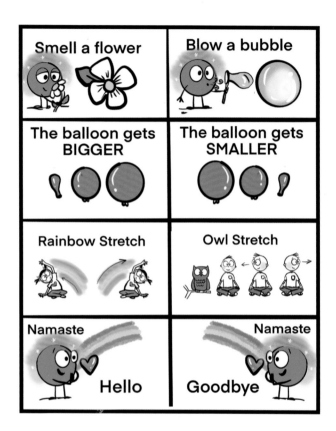

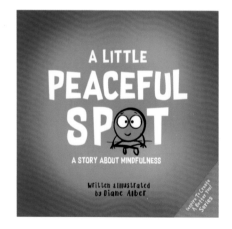

Check out the companion book,
"A Little Peaceful SPOT" and
these printables on
www.dianealber.com